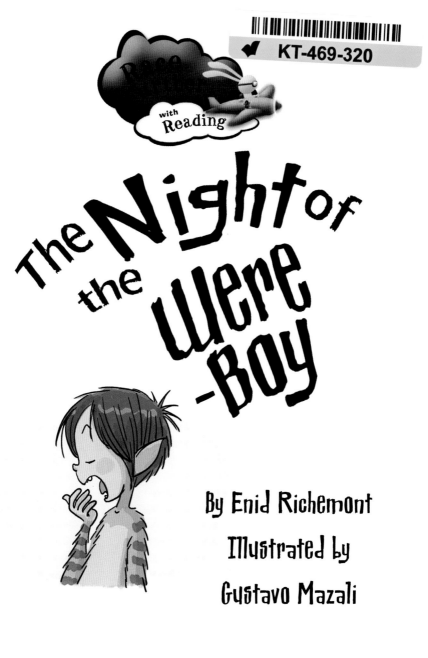

Race Ahead with Reading

The Night of the Were-Boy

By Enid Richemont

Illustrated by

Gustavo Mazali

W

FRANKLIN WATTS

LONDON•SYDNEY

CHAPTER 1
Full Moon

The full moon was drawing patterns
on the kitchen floor. Frankie opened one
eye. Who had switched that light on?
He yawned. Then he stretched and rolled
over, curling his tail around his head.
Moonlight slowly slithered round the rim
of his basket. Frankie stirred and shivered.
Something was wrong.

He uncurled and went to check on his bowl.

His food smelt funny.

His food smelt wrong.

He backed away from the nasty pong.

Then he lapped up some milk from

his yellow saucer.

Yuk, thought Frankie, this food tastes funny. No wonder he felt odd. No wonder he felt strange. No wonder his paws were itching and twitching.

He tried licking them better, but all at once they started to grow. They grew, and they grew. "Meeeaow!" howled Frankie.

Then from his front paws popped out ten stubby fingers, and from his back paws popped out ten stubby toes. Frankie stared down at them. "S-s-s-s-s!" he hissed.

Suddenly he itched all over. He quivered, and crackled, and his head shot up higher than the table top. Frankie staggered about on his new long back legs. The floor was so far down, it made him feel dizzy.

And a **WORD** came jumping out of his new stretchy mouth.

"**Help!**" Frankie heard it.

"Meeeaow!" he wailed.

"**HELP?**"

CHAPTER 2
Fingers and Toes

Frankie's owner, Martin, came into the kitchen. He switched on the light. Then his mouth fell open.

"Who are you?" gasped Martin.

"I'm Frankie," wailed Frankie.

"And I'm not well."

Martin frowned at the empty cat basket.

"And where's my cat?"

"I'm your cat," howled Frankie.

But Martin just looked cross.

"What?" he pointed. "Because you've dyed
your hair and got no clothes on? Bet you're
a burglar! And a cat-napper." Martin
backed away. "I'm getting my dad."

Frankie tried to jump into his basket,

but he was much too big.

"I *am* your cat," he sniffed, getting up.

"Some cat!" sneered Martin. "With arms?

And legs? And fingers and toes?"

He pointed. "So where are your whiskers?

Where's your tail?"

"Here," said Frankie. "Look!" He tried to
show off his tail, but there wasn't any tail.
He tried to lick the fur on his tummy.

He spread out his
front claws, and ten
flat fingernails.

He tried to scratch
behind his ear with
his five stubby toes.

No tail.

No claws.

No whiskers!

"I'm a monster!" shrieked Frankie.

"OH, MEEEAOW!"

Martin looked even more cross.

"Stop making those stupid cat noises,"

he complained. "It's not funny."

Frankie nibbled between his fingers to comfort himself.

"What have you done with my cat?" demanded Martin.

"Nothing," Frankie whimpered. Then he stole a piece of cake from a plate on the table. Perhaps cake would make his tail grow back.

"Bad cat!" said Martin, without thinking.

"You called me a cat!" crowed Frankie.

"Didn't!"

"Yes, you did!"

"Didn't, didn't, didn't!"

protested Martin.

"Did! Did! DID!"

Frankie tried to purr. Then he sidled up

to Martin, and lifted his chin.

"Scratch me there," he said.

"Scratch yourself," growled Martin.

Then Frankie suddenly remembered something. "Butter," he said, and his mouth began to water. "You let me lick it off your fingers when your mum's not looking."

Martin goggled. That was a secret between him and his cat.

CHAPTER 3
The Were-Boy

Frankie was beginning to enjoy himself.

Words were more fun than catnip mice.

He played with some more.

"Remember when I got stuck under the

floorboards?" he said. "I was chasing a

spider. Your dad nearly nailed me in."

"You can't be Frankie," cried Martin. "You're just some stupid boy." But, he wondered, how could a burglar know about that? "And your friend's little sister always pulls my tail," Frankie said. That was true, too. "You haven't got a tail," said Martin weakly.

Suddenly he noticed the big round moon. Could that be it? he wondered. Like in that scary film on TV where the moon makes a man turn into a wolf? Could it work the other way? Had the full moon turned Frankie into something else? Not a wolf, but a **boy?** He grinned. They called the man a were-wolf, he remembered. Did that make his cat a were-**boy?**

"I think you might have been turned into

a were-boy," Martin said slowly.

"A what-boy?" asked Frankie.

"A were-boy," said Martin.

"Like a were-wolf, **you** know."

Frankie shook his head.

"No, I don't," he said.

"In the story," Martin told him, "this man gets changed into a wolf each time there's a full moon. Then, when the moon goes down, he gets changed back." He pointed. "Well, there's a full moon tonight."

"So what?" Frankie yawned. "I'm a cat."

"Maybe cats can get changed into other things, too."

Frankie pulled a face.

"A wolf would be OK," he grumbled.

"I wouldn't mind being a wolf. But who wants to look like a **boy?** Yuk!"

Then he suddenly thought of something.

Boys, thought Frankie, may not have fur.

They may not have tails or proper

whiskers...but they are people. And people

own all the tins of cat food. They own

all the cream, butter and milk.

A were-boy? thought Frankie.

This was going to be fun.

He tried opening the fridge, using his
new thumb and his four new fingers.
Inside was a feast. Frankie dribbled. He
pulled out a chicken leg and some leftover
chocolate pudding. He dropped them into
his bowl.

"I'm cooking," boasted Frankie.

"I've watched your mum, and I know what
to do. You just have to stir things and mix
things up." So that is just what he did.

Frankie squatted on the floor and began to eat. "Yuk!" he yelled. "This tastes awful!" Martin patted his head.

"Poor old Frankie!" He picked up the bowl. "Come on. Let's clear up this mess, or Mum will be mad!"

"It's **not** a mess." Frankie looked hurt. "And what do you mean, poor Frankie? I'm a boy now, so I'm just as good as you."

"Only until the moon goes down," Martin reminded him. "After that, you'll be my cat Frankie again."

"So what?" sniffed Frankie. "At least I'll have a tail and all my fur." He looked scornfully at Martin. "Not like **some** I could mention."

CHAPTER 4
Garden Intruders

The hairs on Frankie's head suddenly rose.

He looked really scary.

"Enemy outside," he hissed.

Scared, Martin ran to the window. Then he grinned. "It's only Samson," he said.

"On **my** territory?" spat Frankie. He tried to wriggle through the cat flap, but his head got stuck. Martin grabbed him by the waist, and hauled him back. He just couldn't stop laughing.

"Silly Frankie," he said.

Frankie squatted on a pile of old newspapers.

"I want to go out," he sulked.

"Well you can't," said Martin. "Poor Samson! He hasn't done anything to you."

"He's on **my** territory," growled Frankie.

"It's his wall, too," Martin pointed out.

"Got to go out," said Frankie slyly.

"Got to pee."

"OK. You win," sighed Martin.

"But you can't go out like that."

He pulled some jeans and a sweatshirt

out of the laundry basket. "Put these on,"

he said. Frankie pushed his fingers into

the legs of the jeans. He put his feet into

the shirt sleeves.

Martin sorted him out. It took a long time, because Frankie kept wriggling.

"Clothes are stupid!" he grumbled.

"I'd much rather just have fur."

Martin opened the kitchen door, and they went out on to the balcony. Instantly, Samson fled, upsetting all Mum's flower pots.

"Get lost!" hissed Frankie, showing off.

Then he leapt up onto the wall.

Martin was horrified.

"Get off there!" he shouted.

"It's a long way down.

You'll fall!"

Frankie sniffed. "Cats never fall," he said snootily. "And even if they do, they always land on their feet. Anyway, there's a fox down there..." He gave a bloodcurdling howl and began dancing up and down. "Watch out, Foxie!" he yelled. "I'm a were-boy, and I'm coming to get you!"

Martin grabbed his jeans and hauled
Frankie back.

"Shut up!" he whispered. "You'll wake up
the whole building. Anyway, I thought you
came out for a pee." He pointed. "There's
your tray. Go on, do it."

Frankie gawped at the cat litter.

"Too small," he grumbled.

"Can't do it in that."

"**Real** boys," teased Martin, "use the toilet."

"What's a toilet?" asked Frankie.

So Martin explained.

"They do it in the **house**?" howled Frankie.
He looked horrified. "**Real** boys are
so disgusting."

"It'll have to be down in the garden, then."
Martin sighed. "OK, come on."

He took Mum's keys from the hook (she'd be so mad if she knew). He opened the front door and closed it quietly. Then he and Frankie ran down three flights of steps, and into the big garden everyone shared. Moonlight glittered on the grass, and there were big black shadows, but Martin wasn't scared.

This was fun, thought Martin. He was out
with a were-boy. He was out with his cat.
Then Frankie ran off into the bushes. He
must be having a pee, Martin guessed.

He waited politely. He waited a long time.

Was Frankie lost? He began to call:

"Frankie! Frankie!"

A hand came out of the darkness, and

closed around his mouth.

"Shut up, kid," said a voice.

And it wasn't Frankie's.

CHAPTER 5
Were-Boy to the Rescue

A man flashed a torch in Martin's face.

"So where's your little friend?" he whispered.

A second man grabbed Martin's arm.

"We don't like all this noise," he said.

"We're on an important job." He smiled a nasty smile.

"So where's this kid Frankie?" demanded the first man.

Martin shivered. "I don't know."

Something moved in the bushes.

Something rustled, then stopped.

"What was that?" muttered the first man.

His torchlight moved over Martin's old
jeans. "It must be the little kid's friend,
Frankie," he sniggered.

Frankie was crouching in the ivy.
His shoulders were quivering, and his
eyes glowed bright blue.

"What's he up to?" sneered the man.
"Why is he creeping about like a cat?"
"Frankie, run!" yelled Martin. "Go and
get help!" But Frankie just stiffened, and
Frankie just stared.

The first man walked up to him slowly.
"We don't like kids creeping about," he said.
"We get nasty," said the second man,
"very nasty."
But Frankie still didn't move. He just stared.

The man tried to grab him. Then Frankie leapt. His stripey hair bristled, and his nails were like knives.

"Aaaaagh!" yelped the first man.

The second man gaped as the were-boy struck again. "This kid's an **animal!**" he screamed. "Let's get out of here!"

The moon began setting behind the buildings. People were coming outside. "What was all that noise about?" people were saying. Martin heard his dad's voice: "What's going on down there?"

And suddenly, down in the bushes, there was a small, black and white cat.

Martin helped little Frankie out of his tangle of clothes. "Told you," he whispered, pointing up at the sky.

Then Frankie snuggled up against Martin's pyjamas, and put his two front paws against Martin's chest.

A police siren wailed past.

"I hope they catch those two," Martin whispered to Frankie. He quietly unlocked the front door, and tiptoed inside. In the kitchen, he put Frankie back into his basket. Then he took a crust of bread, and spread it with butter. Frankie sniffed. Something smelled tasty. Martin put the bread down next to his bowl.

"For Supercats," he whispered.

"For were-boys. For **you**."

Frankie wriggled down, and came over.

He lapped up some milk. Then he nosed

at his cat food. It smelt quite delicious.

He licked all the butter off the crust of bread.

Then he climbed back inside his basket.

His tummy felt fat, and his whiskers tasted

buttery.

He'd been in a fight, he remembered,

yawning. Had it been Samson? He stretched,

then wound his tail around his head.

Whoever it had been, he knew that he'd won.

It must have been a dream, thought Martin in the morning. A dream that his cat had turned into a boy. Then Mum pointed. "Who made all that mess on my kitchen floor?" she demanded. Martin suddenly saw the sticky trail of chocolate pudding. He shrugged. "Not me."

"Maybe it was burglars," joked Dad.
"They caught a couple in the garden last
night. Someone heard noises in the bushes,
and called the police."

Mum laughed. "The funny thing is –
people say the burglars seemed quite glad
to be caught." Then Martin looked down at
Frankie, and grinned.

'For David Richemont, star-gazer and cat-man.' E.R.

First published in 2014 by
Franklin Watts
338 Euston Road
London
NW1 3BH

Franklin Watts Australia
Level 17/207 Kent Street
Sydney
NSW 2000

Text © Enid Richemont 2014
Illustration © Gustavo Mazali 2014

The rights of Enid Richemont to be
identified as the author and Gustavo Mazali
as the illustrator of this Work have been
asserted in accordance with the Copyright,
Designs and Patents Act, 1988.

Series Editor: Melanie Palmer
Series Advisor: Catherine Glavina
Series Designer: Cathryn Gilbert

A CIP catalogue record for this book is
available from the British Library.

ISBN 978 1 4451 3349 2 (hbk)
ISBN 978 1 4451 3350 8 (pbk)
ISBN 978 1 4451 3351 5 (ebook)
ISBN 978 1 4451 3352 2 (library ebook)

Printed in China

Franklin Watts is a division of Hachette
Children's Books, an Hachette UK company
www.hachette.co.uk